The Gum Chewing Rattler

By Joe Hayes

Illustrated by Antonio Castro L.

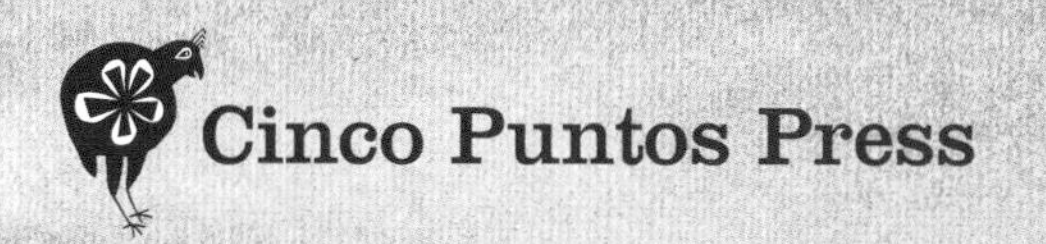

When I was a kid growing up in Arizona, I used to love to chew bubblegum.

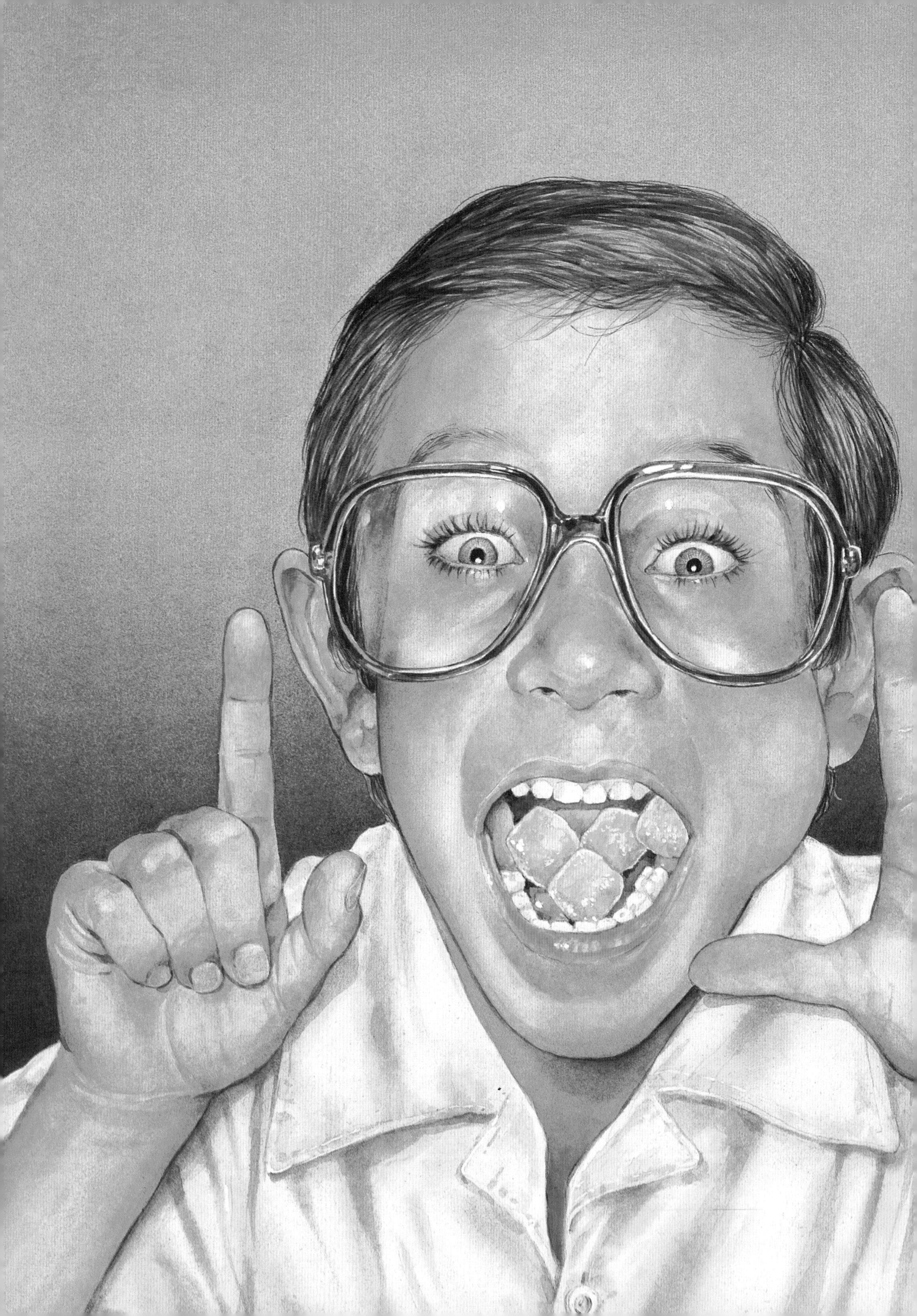

I always had a big, juicy wad of bubblegum in my mouth. I'm not talking about one piece of bubblegum. I would put two or three pieces of gum in my mouth at once. I might even put six or seven pieces of bubblegum in my mouth at the same time!

I would be chomping away on bubblegum all the time—even when I was in school. My teacher would see the wad in my mouth and snap, "Get rid of that gum!" I had to take the gum out of my mouth and wrap it in some paper and throw it in the wastebasket.

I didn't really care. I always kept another package of bubblegum right in my shirt pocket.

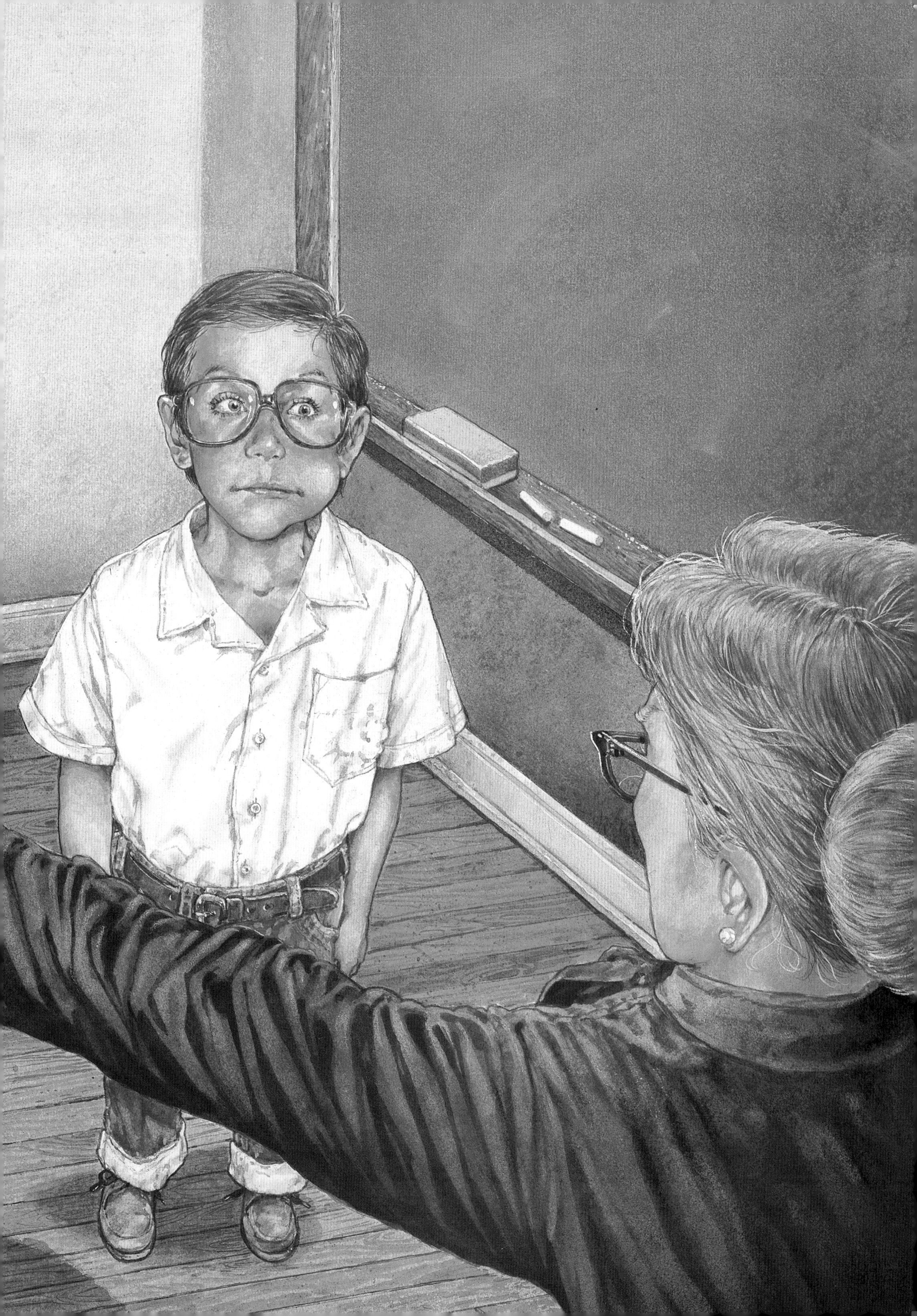

My mom was the one who would really get mad at me though, because I would forget to take the gum out of my shirt pocket. I'd throw my shirt in the wash with all the other dirty clothes.

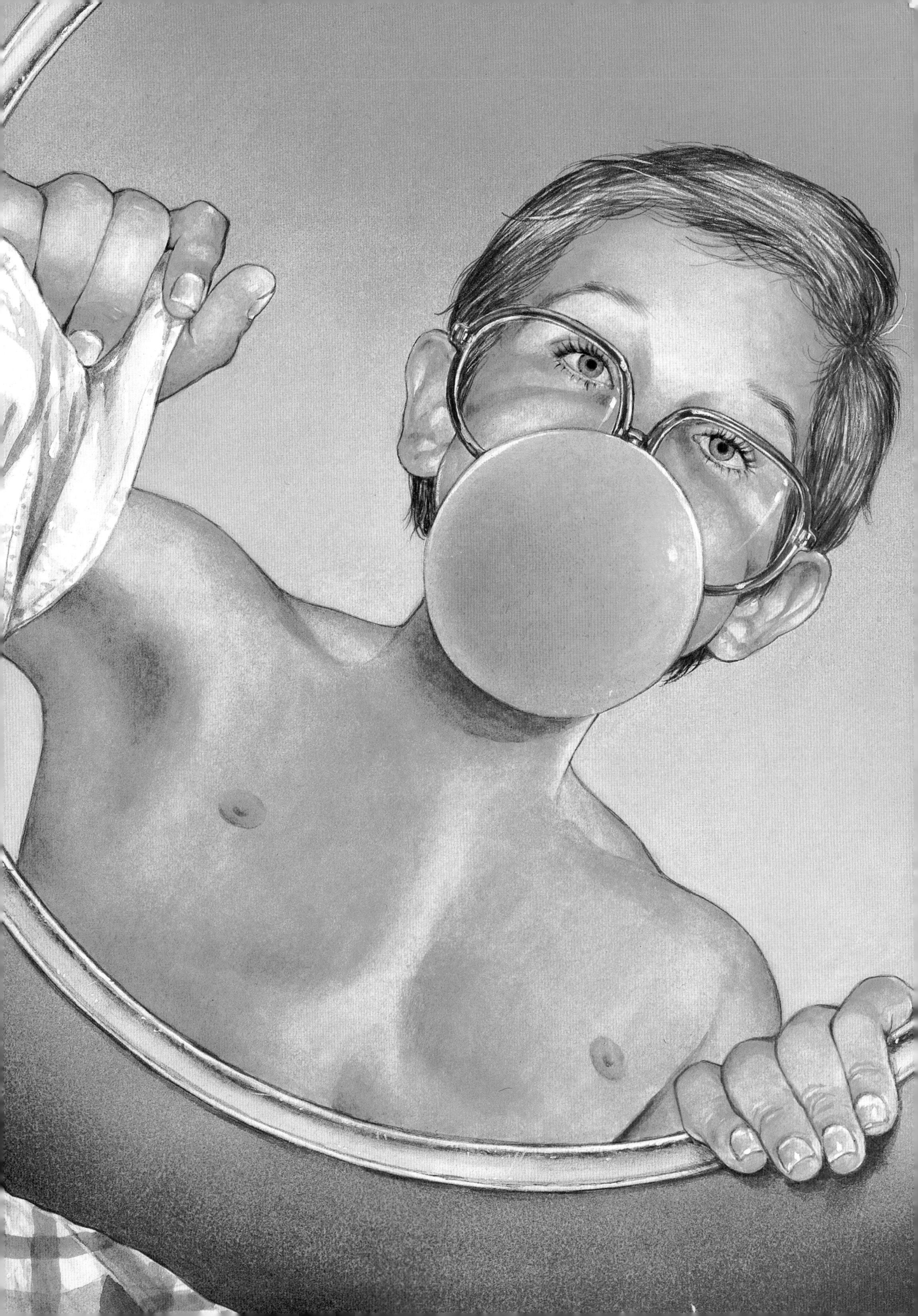

Now, I grew up a very long time ago, and my mom had one of those old-fashioned wringer washing machines. Her washing machine didn't spin. She had to put each piece of clothing through the wringer and the rollers would squeeze the water out. She would put my shirt through the wringer and the rollers would squish the bubblegum right into the cloth and make a big, gunky stain all around the pocket.

My mom would say, "Look at this! You've ruined another shirt!"

But then one day something happened that changed her mind and she never got mad at me again for carrying gum in my shirt pocket.

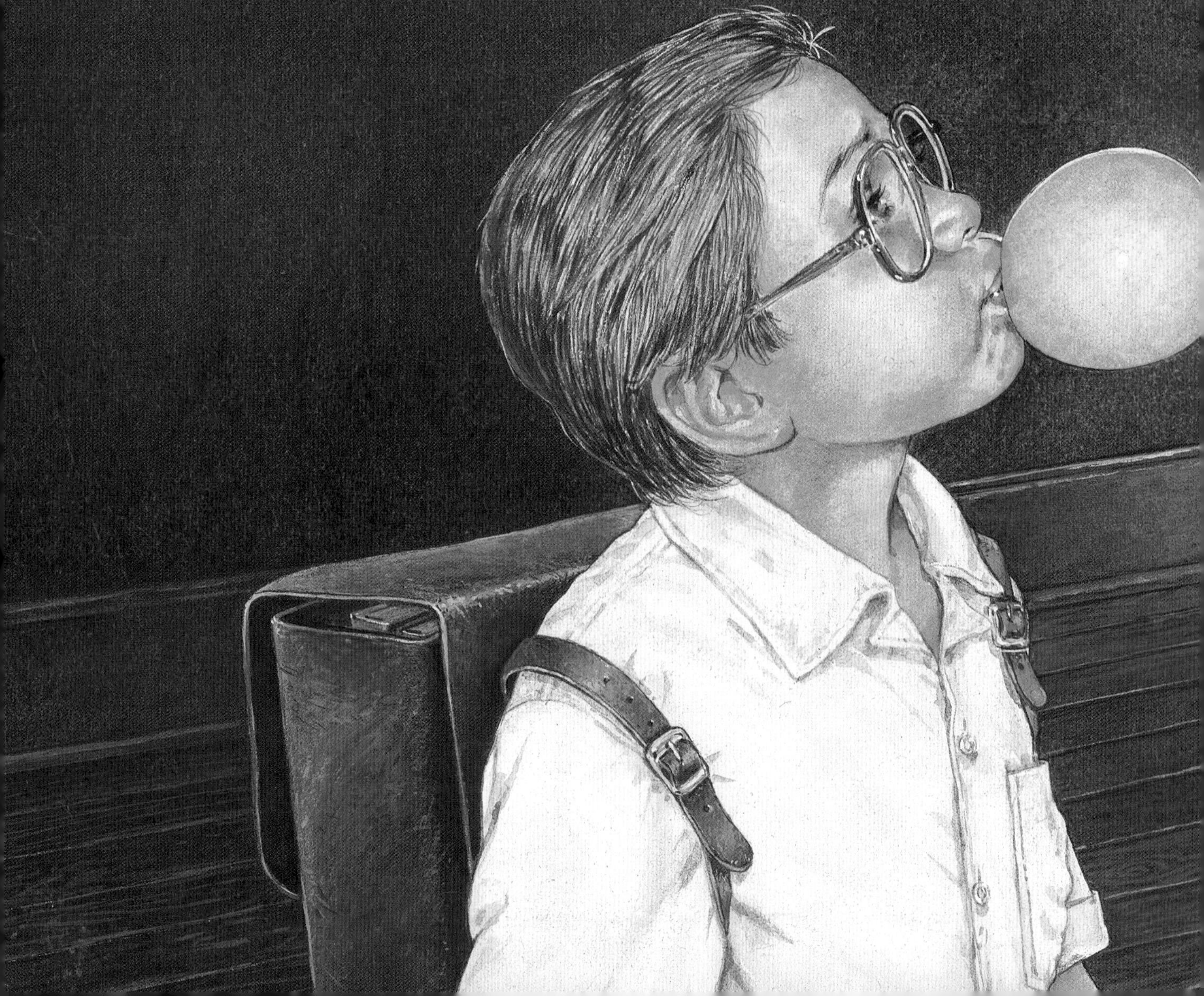

That day I was walking around out in the desert, kind of daydreaming, chomping on my bubblegum and not paying attention to where I was going. And I stepped right on a rattlesnake's tail!

The snake couldn't rattle and warn me because I was standing on his tail. So he didn't even worry about warning me. He just came striking up through the air, aiming his fangs right at my heart. That rattlesnake hit me—**bam!**—right on my shirt pocket. That's where I was carrying my spare bubblegum! And the rattlesnake's fangs stuck in the bubblegum.

There I stood with my foot on the rattlesnake's tail and with his fangs stuck in my shirt pocket. He was thrashing around and whipping up against me. I was so scared I couldn't even move. I just froze there, staring into his beady little eyes.

Those eyes were just looking hate back at me. The snake started working his jaws all around, trying to get his fangs out of the gum so that he could get back at me and really bite me good!

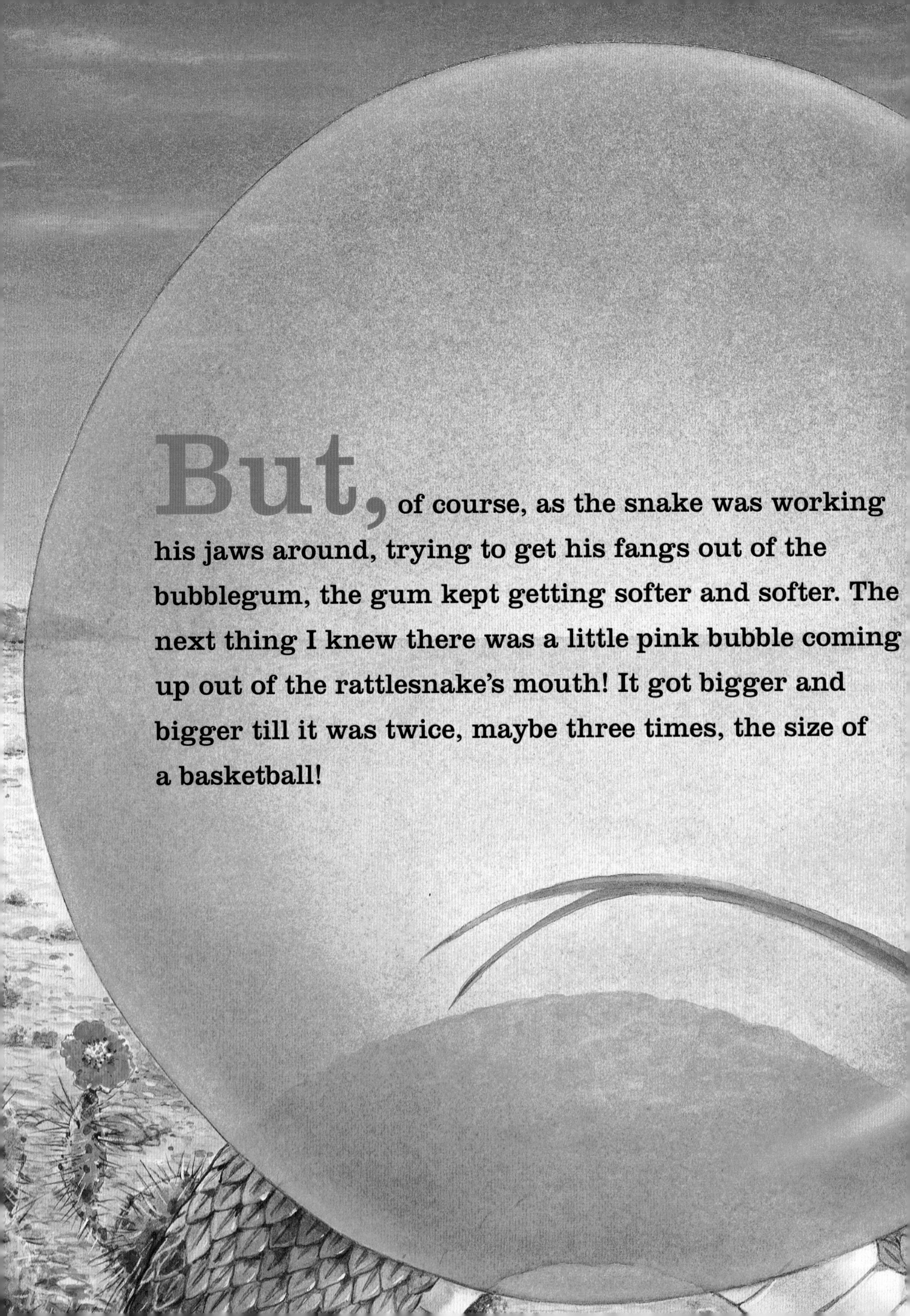

But, of course, as the snake was working his jaws around, trying to get his fangs out of the bubblegum, the gum kept getting softer and softer. The next thing I knew there was a little pink bubble coming up out of the rattlesnake's mouth! It got bigger and bigger till it was twice, maybe three times, the size of a basketball!

I got up all my courage. I brought my hand up slowly and—**pop!**—I broke the bubble. The snake went flying back and his head hit on a rock and it knocked him out cold!

But that did take all my courage. I fainted. I fell out in the other direction.

I didn't come home for lunch and my mom came looking for me. She found me lying there on the ground. And lying in the other direction was a rattlesnake with bubblegum all over his face.

My mom asked me what had happened, and I told her the same story I just told **you**. You know what?

She didn't believe it.
Did you?

Photo by Francisco X. Dominguez

Artist Antonio Castro L. looking at photos with Lynn Coyle and Lynn's daughter Oriana Dominguez. Lynn served as the model for Joe Hayes' mother in THE GUM-CHEWING RATTLER and Oriana fell out flat on the floor so Antonio could capture what happens when a person tangles with a rattler.

Photo by Clara G. Urias Castro

Antonio Castro's grandson José Arturo Urias Castro let his mouth drop open so he could pose as young Joe when he encounterered a rattlesnake.

Antonio Castro L. uses real people as his models when he illustrates so he can capture all their emotions and feelings. First he takes photos; later he illustrates, using the photo as his guide. Thanks then to Lynn Coyle, Oriana Dominguez, and José Arturo Urias Castro for their outstanding performances as models for Joe's very tall tale!

Printed in Hong Kong. Thanks, Suzy.

FIRST EDITION

10 9 8 7 6 5 4 3 2 1

Library of Congress Cataloging-in-Publication Data

Hayes, Joe.
The gum-chewing rattler / as told by Joe Hayes ; illustrated by Antonio Castro L. -- 1st ed.
p. cm.
Summary: A tall tale of a boy whose chewing gum habit saves him from a rattlesnake's bite.
ISBN: 978-1-933693-19-4
[1. Chewing gum--Fiction. 2. Rattlesnakes--Fiction. 3. Snakes--Fiction. 4. Tall tales.] I. Castro Lopez, Antonio, ill. II. Title.
PZ7.H31474Gum 2006
[E]--dc22
2006017602

Book and cover design by Antonio Castro H.